MAGIC
BONE

DOGS DON'T HAVE
WEBBED FEET

GROSSET & DUNLAP
Published by the Penguin Group
Penguin Group (USA) LLC, 375 Hudson Street, New York, New York 10014, USA

USA | Canada | UK | Ireland | Australia | New Zealand | India | South Africa | China

penguin.com
A Penguin Random House Company

Text copyright © 2015 by Nancy Krulik.
Illustrations copyright © 2015 by Sebastien Braun. All rights reserved.
Published by Grosset & Dunlap, a division of Penguin Young Readers Group,
345 Hudson Street, New York, New York 10014. GROSSET & DUNLAP is a
trademark of Penguin Group (USA) LLC. Printed in the USA.

Library of Congress Cataloging-in-Publication Data is available.

ISBN 978-0-448-48096-1   1 0 9 8 7 6 5 4 3

MAGIC BONE

DOGS DON'T HAVE WEBBED FEET

by Nancy Krulik
illustrated by Sebastien Braun

Grosset & Dunlap
An Imprint of Penguin Group (USA) LLC

For Bonnie Bader, editor extraordinaire, who helps keep Sparky from *kabooming* too far off track—NK

For Matheus—SB

CHAPTER 1

"Throw the ball!" I bark. "Throw the ball! THROW THE BALL!"

My paws bounce up and down in the cold snow each time I bark. They love playing fetch. My tail wags wildly. *It* loves playing fetch, too.

"Throw the ball!" I bark again.

My two-leg, Josh, finally throws the bright white ball across our yard. It is heading straight for Josh's two-leg friend, Sophie. But I'm faster than she is. Before Sophie can catch the ball, I leap up, open my mouth, and grab it in midair.

Wiggle, waggle, weird. The ball is melting in my mouth. It's not a ball anymore. It's icy-cold water. This isn't a fetch ball—it's a *snow*ball!

I don't like this kind of ball. I can't run it back to Josh. And he can't pick it up and throw it again. Snowballs are definitely not made for playing fetch.

But Josh and Sophie are still playing with the snowballs.

Bam! A snowball hits Sophie. It explodes. Now it isn't a ball anymore. It's just snow.

Josh bends over and starts to make another ball.

Bash! Sophie throws a ball right at the place Josh's tail would be—if he had a tail. It explodes all over him.

Josh smiles and laughs. But he doesn't throw a ball back at Sophie.

I guess Josh and Sophie have gotten tired of throwing balls that can't be fetched, because now they are walking toward the gate. I follow right behind them.

"Where are we going?" I bark to Josh. "Are we going to play a new game? Are we going to play fetch the stick? Are we going to play chew the sock?"

The last time I played chew the sock, Josh got angry. I don't know why. It's so much fun to chew on a sock. Especially one that smells like Josh's feet.

"Sparky, stay!" Josh says. He holds up his hand.

I know what *stay* means. It means
I have to stand still, even though Josh
and Sophie are walking away.

Josh and Sophie leave the yard.
They close the gate. A minute later
I hear a rumbling noise. The noise
starts out loud. Then it gets quieter
and quieter.

I know what that means. Josh and
Sophie have gone away in his metal

machine with the four round paws.

Sometimes Josh takes me to fun places like the park or the dog-toy store in his metal machine. But today I have to stay here while Josh and Sophie visit fun places.

Wiggle, waggle, boo! Two-legs have all the fun.

Well, not *all* the fun. I can go places, too. And I don't need a metal machine to do it. All I need is my magic bone.

My magic bone is amazing. One big bite and *kaboom!* I go far, far away. Like that time my magic bone *kaboomed* me all the way to Tokyo, Japan. I got to eat squishy fishy called sashimi with some Ninja Dogs. And I got to fight like a sumo wrestler!

Another time my magic bone *kaboomed* me to London, England. I played ball with a two-leg in Covent Garden, and I helped my friend Watson find a *fur*ever home, like the one I have with Josh.

Then there was the time I visited Zermatt, Switzerland. The wind and the snow were very, very cold. But the cheese was melty and hot. *Really* hot. It burned my tongue. Lucky for me, there was lots of icy-cold snow to lick. Here's something I learned in Zermatt: Never, *ever* lick the yellow snow.

My magic bone has taken me many places. But the best place it takes me is right here—to my own house. I like going on adventures.

But I *love* coming home again. I'm glad that whenever I've had enough adventuring, I can take another bite of my bone and come back here.

But Josh isn't home right now. Which means it's a great time for a magic-bone adventure.

I hurry over to my favorite digging spot, where Josh grows his flowers. There aren't any flowers there now.

Only snow. But under the snow, there's lots of dirt. And that's where I've buried my magic bone.

I *diggety, dig, dig* in the dirt. It flies everywhere.

There it is. My magic bone. My bright, beautiful, sparkly magic bone. Sitting right in the middle of the hole.

Sniffety, sniff, sniff. My bone smells good. Like chicken, beef, and sausage all rolled into one.

I just *have* to take a bite . . . Chomp!

Wiggle, waggle, whew. I feel

dizzy—like my insides are spinning all around—but my outsides are standing still. Stars are twinkling in front of my eyes—even though it's daytime! All around me I smell food— fried chicken, salmon, roast beef. But there isn't any food in sight.

And then . . .

Kaboom! Kaboom! Kaboom!

CHAPTER 2

It sure is hot here.

There's no snow under my paws now. Only dirt. Squooshy, mushy, wet dirt. The kind of dirt that's fun to roll around in.

Roll, roll, roll! I love rolling around in squooshy, mushy, wet dirt.

Roll, roll . . . Ow! A bug just stung me.

Scratchity, scratch, scratch.

Aaaahhh. That's better. Thank you, back paw.

Birds are tweeting all around me. I look up. But I can't see the birds. They must be in the treetops. It's way too high for me to see.

I'm going to bury my bone right next to this tall, tall tree. When I'm ready to go home, I will know just where to find it.

Diggety, dig, dig.

I drop my bone into the hole and push the dirt back over it. Now my bone is completely hidden. I'm the only one who knows where it is. Well, me and the bug that's buzzing near my ear. Lucky for me, bugs can't dig.

Owie, ow, ow! But bugs *can* sting.

"Hey! That hurt." I bat the bug away with my paw. The bug buzzes off. He's scared of me. I'm a lot bigger than he is.

But even *I* feel little around here. Everything in this place seems huge—except for the bugs. The flowers are gigantic. The bushes are so thick you can't look through them. The trees are so tall you can't see their tops. And . . .

Hey! Look at that!

It's a big black-and-white ball. Wow! Even the balls are bigger in this place!

"I wanna play ball!" I bark to the two-legs who are playing with the big black-and-white ball. "I love fetch."

Except the two-legs aren't playing fetch. They're moving the ball with their *paws*.

I run over to the ball. I stick out one paw and try to push the big ball, just like the two-legs are doing.

Whoops! It's hard to balance on three legs. I fall right onto my belly. Owie! That hurt.

A two-leg pushes the ball away. He passes it to another two-leg, who

pushes it down the field of soft grass.

"Wait for me!" I shout to the two-leg as I try to reach the ball.

The two-leg stops and stares at me. Now's my chance. I stick out my snout and push that ball away.

The two-leg shouts something at me. But I can't understand him. I don't speak two-leg. So I keep pushing the ball with my snout.

A group of two-legs chases after me.

I push harder. I run faster. This is a fun game!

I push the ball into some squooshy, mushy, wet dirt that's covered with flowers and bushes. I push it around a big, fallen piece of tree and through a puddle of water. *Splash!*

"You can't catch me!" I bark to the two-legs as I run.

The two-legs aren't giving up. They run after me, trying to get the ball.

We all run and run and run. I can't see the field anymore. All I see are trees and bushes and flowers.

I keep pushing the ball.

The two-legs keep chasing me.

Push. Push.

Chase. Chase.

HOOONNNNNNKKKKKK!

Just then I hear a really loud noise. I look up from the ball in time to see a huge metal machine with giant round paws heading right for me!

Wiggle, waggle, uh-oh! I leap into the bushes.

HOOONNNNNNKKKKKK! The metal machine squawks again.

"AAAAHHHHH!" the two-legs behind me shout.

The metal machine swerves and . . . CRASH! It bangs right into a big pile of rocks. It stops.

Phew. That was close.

A big two-leg climbs out of the metal machine. He yells at the group of two-legs who were playing the ball game with me. The group of ball-playing two-legs shouts back at him.

There is a whole lot of yelling going on. I can't understand what any of the two-legs are saying. But I can tell that they are angry.

The big two-leg stomps off, leaving his metal machine crushed up against the rocks.

Another two-leg picks up the big black-and-white ball. He walks away. His friends follow him. Now I'm alone in this strange land of giant trees, flowers, and metal machines.

I don't see any other dogs around here, which means I don't have anyone to talk to. And now that all those two-legs have taken their ball and gone away, I don't have anyone to play with, either.

I have lots of friends at home. Like Frankie and Samson, the dogs who live on the other sides of my fence. I can talk to them. And there's Josh, too. Maybe he will come home soon and play with me.

I think I'll go home now. That's where all the fun is!

I start walking back toward the big tree where I buried my magic bone.

"There he is! There's our hero!"

Suddenly I stop in my tracks. My head whips around. I look everywhere. But I don't see anyone.

"Who's there?" I ask nervously.

No one answers.

Then a furry brown dog pops out from behind a big tree.

At least I *think* she's a dog. She has a furry body and a bushy tail, just like dogs do. And she speaks dog, too.

But her paws don't look like dog paws. They look more like the paws I see on the ducks that live in the pond near my house. Except her paws have claws like mine do.

I turn around.

Uh-oh. Now I'm surrounded by duck-pawed dog creatures! *Four* of them. And they're all staring at me.

I look at their tails. And their ears. And then back at their paws. My heart starts *thumpety, thump, thumping.*

What kind of strange four-legs are these?

And what do they want with me?

CHAPTER 3

"Where are you going?" the largest of the duck-pawed dog creatures asks me. He scratches his ear with one of his duck paws.

Gulp. Those paws really freak me out. "I . . . um . . . I was just leaving," I tell him. "I don't want any trouble."

"Oh, there won't be any trouble," another one of the duck-pawed dog creatures assures me. She wags her tail. "Not since you scared away the two-leg and saved our home. You're our hero."

Saved their home? I don't see any houses anywhere. "What home?" I ask.

The largest of the duck-pawed dog creatures points to a huge pile of dried grass. "That's our lair," he tells me.

"Your what?" I ask.

"Our lair," another duck-pawed dog creature with a loud voice repeats. She shakes her head. "Haven't you ever seen a bush-dog house before?"

I've heard of sheepdogs, collie dogs, terrier dogs, beagle dogs, spaniel dogs, even mixed-breed dogs. But I've never heard of bush dogs.

"What's a bush dog?" I ask.

The duck-pawed dog creatures look at me like I'm crazy.

"*We're* bush dogs," the loudest one tells me. "And this is our home."

That doesn't look like any house I've ever seen. "Where are the windows and the doors?" I ask her.

"What's a door?" she asks me.

"What's a window?" the one with the wagging tail asks.

"Our lair used to belong to an armadillo," the biggest one explains. "When he moved out, we moved in."

I don't know what an armadillo is. This place is very confusing.

"We're so happy you saved our home," the bush dog with the wagging tail exclaims. "You're our hero!"

"My name's not Hero," I tell her. "It's Sparky."

"Hi, Sparky," she says. "I'm Anahi."

Anahi smells my rear end. I guess she really is a dog, because that's how we dogs say hello.

"I'm Tito," the big duck-pawed dog tells me. He smells my rear end, too. Then he points to one of his friends.

"This is Eduardo. He doesn't say much."

Eduardo nods his head in my direction and gives me a little sniff.

"Hi," I say.

"I'm Maria," the dog with the loud voice says. She gives me a funny look. "Are you really a dog?" she asks.

"Yes," I say proudly.

"You don't look like one," Maria says.

"I was just thinking the same thing," Tito agrees. "It's the paws. You have strange paws, hero."

"Sparky," I correct him. "And my paws aren't strange. They look normal where I come from."

"Where is that?" Anahi asks.

"Josh's house," I say.

Eduardo cocks his head and looks at Tito.

"He wants to know what a Josh is," Tito explains.

"Josh is my two-leg," I tell Eduardo.

The duck-pawed dogs all step back.

"You brought a two-leg to the rain forest?" Maria shouts. She sounds kind of angry.

"The rain forest? I don't see any rain," I say. "Or is that the name of this place?"

"We're in the Amazon Rain Forest," Tito explains. "In Brazil."

"If Sparky brought a two-leg here, we could be in trouble," Maria warns the others.

"Josh isn't here," I tell them. "He went off in his metal machine."

"We HATE metal machines," Maria says. "And we don't like the two-legs inside them, either."

"You wouldn't say that if you knew

Josh," I explain. "He's *wiggle, waggle, wonderful!*"

Eduardo lifts one paw and shakes his head.

"Eduardo's not sure he can trust a dog with weird paws," Tito tells me. "Especially one who is friends with a two-leg."

That makes me angry. "*Your* paws look weird to *me*," I tell Eduardo. "Maybe I shouldn't trust *you*."

"We trust you," Anahi assures me. "It's two-legs we don't trust. They haven't been very good to us bush dogs."

"They plowed over our last two homes," Tito explains. "Luckily this time you stopped them."

"That's why you're our hero!" Anahi explains. "From now on, you're the leader of our pack."

"Ow!" I exclaim. "A bug just bit me." My back paw scratches at the bug bite. *Scratchity, scratch, scratch.*

"It was just a mosquito," Maria says. "You'll get used to them."

No, I won't. Because I'm not

staying here. It's great having other dogs to talk to, but the rest of this place is just too much. Too much yelling from two-legs. Too much heat. And too much biting from the bugs.

Ow! Another bug bites me. *Scratchity, scratch, scratch.*

And all this heat is making me thirsty. The air seems really wet, but I don't see a water bowl anywhere.

"It was nice meeting you," I tell the bush dogs. "But I have to go home now."

"You can't leave," Anahi says. "You have to stay and be our leader."

Eduardo nods.

But I don't answer. Instead, I start walking back toward the big tree where my bone is buried. The bush dogs follow me as I walk.

"Where are you going?" I ask them.

"Wherever *you're* going," Anahi tells me. "We're following the leader."

"You can't go where I'm going," I tell her.

Eduardo cocks his head.

"He wants to know why not," Tito says.

I don't know what to say. I can't tell the bush dogs that Josh and I could never fit four more dogs in our house. That would be rude.

Crash!

Suddenly, I hear a loud noise. The ground shakes. *I* shake. It's the scariest sound I've ever heard.

"Oh no!" Anahi exclaims. "There goes another one."

"Another what?" I ask her.

Eduardo looks up.

"Tree," Tito tells me.

"The two-legs keep knocking them down and flattening the land," Maria says. "I don't know what they do with all those trees. But I do know a bunch of birds just lost their home."

That's so sad. I don't know what I'd do if someone knocked down my house.

CRASH!

"Stop knocking down birds' houses!" I shout to the metal machines. They don't answer. Metal machines don't talk.

But they do knock down trees. I don't want to be here when they do that again. So I run toward the tall,

tall tree that stands near where I buried my bone.

Run. Run. Run.

Fast. Faster . . .

Oh no! This is *baddy, bad, bad*!

The tree is gone. *All* the trees are gone. So are the plants. There's nothing here but flat, smooth dirt. "Where's the tall, tall tree?" I ask nervously. "It was here before."

"It could have been the tree we heard fall," Tito tells me.

"Or one of the other ones," Maria says. "See? The metal machines knocked them all down."

I look around. Sure enough, there are lots of metal machines knocking down trees and chopping them into little pieces.

"Are you sure this is where you buried your bone?" Anahi asks me.

That's just the problem. I'm *not* sure. Everything looks so different here now.

"I don't know," I tell her. "I thought it was. But I don't see the field where two-legs were pushing the big black-and-white ball."

"Those metal machines could have dug up a field," Maria says. "They dig faster than any dog."

Uh-oh! What if one of those metal machines digs up my magic bone? What if one of the two-legs gets his paws on it? What if a two-leg takes a bite of it?

My heart is *thumpety, thump, thumping* hard.

"Don't be sad," Anahi says. "We can get you another bone."

"Not like *my* bone," I say. "It's . . . special." *And I can't get back home without it.*

CHAPTER 4

The bush dogs look at me curiously. I know that they don't understand what's so special about my bone. But I don't have time to explain. I have to start digging. I have to find my bone before those metal machines do.

Diggety, dig, dig. Dirt flies out everywhere.

I dig hole after hole after hole.

But my bone is nowhere.

"Where are you, bone?" I whimper sadly.

Eduardo shakes his head and flops down onto his belly.

"He thinks you should stop and take a break," Tito tells me.

"I can't stop," I insist. "I want to go home."

Anahi nuzzles my ear with her snout. "This can be your new home. You'll love living here with us in the rain forest."

I open my mouth to tell Anahi that my home is with Josh, but before I can even get the words out . . .

Grumble. Rumble. My tummy interrupts me.

I know what it's saying, because I speak tummy. And right now, my tummy is telling me it's hungry.

Sniffety, sniff, sniff. Suddenly, my

nose smells something sweet and fruity. Kind of like the fruit I ate that time my magic bone *kaboomed* me to Hawaii.

Grumble. Rumble.

"Okay, tummy," I say. "I'll get you some fruit."

"Great idea, Sparky," Tito says. "I could go for some food."

"You can *always* go for some food," Maria points out.

"Because I'm *always* hungry," Tito explains. "I'm in the mood to eat a big, fat agouti."

"Yum!" Anahi agrees.

Eduardo wags his tail and licks his lips.

"You're going to love Amazonian food," Tito tells me. "You haven't lived until you've snacked on agouti!"

"Oh no, I'm not eating that," I tell Tito a few minutes later.

"But it's fresh agouti," Tito says. "It's delicious."

The bush dogs have hunted down a little animal. It looks like the squirrels that run around in the yard I share with Josh. I mean the yard I *used* to share with Josh.

Either way, I'm not eating the agouti. No way.

"Here, have some guava," Anahi says. She rolls a green fruit toward me. "It's sweet. Just like you." Her tail wags happily.

I don't know why she thinks *I'm*

sweet. She's never tasted me. "Um . . . thanks," I say as I sink my teeth deep into the round, green fruit.

My nose wrinkles. I don't think it's sweet. Actually, it's sour. My nose doesn't like it. And my mouth doesn't like it, either.

My teeth tear away the sour green part of the guava. My tongue licks at the pink part inside.

Mmmm. The pink part is *yummy, yum, yum!* My tail wags as my teeth sink deeper into the sweetness.

"Who wants to go for a swim?" Tito asks. He swallows his last bite of agouti meat and runs toward some water that is flowing nearby.

"Last one in is a rotten agouti!" Maria exclaims loudly. She runs off at top speed, trying to beat Tito to the water.

Eduardo leaps up. His tail spins around and around. He runs after her.

"Come on, Sparky," Anahi says. She nudges me a little. "Let's go play in the river."

I'm not in the mood to play. But I don't want to sit here all alone, either. So I follow her to the water.

Run. Run. Run.

Run. Run. *SPLASH!*

The water is cool. It's not salty like the water in the Pacific Ocean in Hawaii.

"Come on, Sparky, swim!" Maria shouts. Her paws go back and forth, and she starts moving really fast.

The other bush dogs swim faster, too. They are trying to catch up with her.

I move my paws back and forth. But I can't swim like the bush dogs do. I'm moving slowly. Really slowly.

The bush dogs are splashing and laughing.

But I'm just *paddle, paddle, paddling*.

All this paddling is making me tired. I stop for a minute and climb up onto a big log. I lie down. I roll over. I scratch my back on the log.

Scratchity, scratch, scratch. That feels better. *Scratchity, scratch, scra—*

"SPARKY, NO!"

"Get down from there!" I hear Anahi shout.

I turn over and leap off the log— just *as it opens its mouth*!

Wiggle, waggle, what? A log with teeth. Big, sharp teeth.

Logs aren't supposed to have teeth! But this one does. And those teeth look ready to take a great big bite . . . out of me!

CHAPTER 5

Help! I don't want to get caught by a dog-eating log with giant sharp teeth. And paws.

Logs aren't supposed to have paws. But this one does. *Strong* paws that help it swim fast.

"Come on," I tell *my* paws. "Move it!"

Finally, I reach the squooshy, mushy, wet dirt. I climb out of the river and start to run. Fast. Faster. *Fastest*. My paws work better on land than in water.

The log's paws don't work as well on land. It slows down.

But I don't. I keep running.

Wet fur flies in front of my eyes. I can't see a thing. But I keep going. Fast. Faster. *Whoops!* I trip over some big, thick tree roots. I topple onto my back.

Ouch! That hurt! Stupid tree roots. Stupid fur in my eyes.

I roll over and run a little farther. I have to make sure that log can't catch me.

Finally, I turn around. The dog-eating log has gone away. He's climbing back into the water. He's not going to eat me after all. Phew!

"I beat you, dog-eating log!" I cheer.

The next thing I know, I'm surrounded by bush dogs. Maria, Anahi, and Eduardo have all come out of the water to check on me.

Eduardo tilts his head.

"He wants to know if you're okay," Maria explains.

"Yeah, I'm fine," I tell Eduardo.

"Why would you want to sit on a crocodile?" Anahi wonders.

"A *what*?" I ask her.

"A crocodile," Anahi says again. "You know, that big monster you were scratching your back on."

"I thought that was a log," I say.

The bush dogs laugh.

"You've got a lot to learn if you're going to be living in the Amazon Rain Forest," Maria tells me.

My tail droops between my legs.

Just then, Tito comes running out of the water.

"You couldn't have shared a little of that fish with us?" Maria asks him.

"What fish?" Tito says. "I didn't catch a fish."

"Oh really," Maria says. "Then what's that fish tail doing hanging out of your mouth?"

We all look at Tito. I laugh a little, even though I'm sad to still be in the rain forest. It's hard *not* to laugh at a duck-pawed dog with a fish tail hanging out of his mouth.

Tito swallows the last bit of fish. "I was still hungry," he says. "Agoutis are small. Not much meat on them." He looks up in the tree. "There are some yummy-looking figs up there. I wish we could reach them. They'd make a great dessert."

I don't know what a fig is. But I do know what yummy means. So I look up in the tree, too.

Wiggle, waggle, weird. Suddenly I'm staring right into the face of another dog. Except this dog is hanging upside down from a tree branch.

"How do you do that?" I ask the upside-down dog.

But the upside-down dog doesn't answer.

"Doesn't it hurt your paws?" I bark, a little louder this time.

The upside-down dog spreads his wings and flies away.

Wiggle, waggle, wait a minute. Wings? Flying?

"What kind of dog is *that*?" I ask the bush dogs.

Eduardo laughs. He shakes his head.

"He says that's not a dog. It's a bat," Tito explains.

"A bat?" I repeat. "What's that?"

"It's kind of like a bird, because it flies," Maria explains. "But it doesn't lay eggs."

"It sure had a dog face," I say.

"I guess that's why it's called a bulldog bat," Anahi explains.

I don't want to live in a place that has logs that bite and bulldogs that fly. I want to live with a nice two-leg. One that loves me as much as I love him.

Josh.

That settles it. I'm not giving up. I'm going to find my magic bone. Even if I have to dig up every bit of the rain forest to do it!

CHAPTER 6

"Some leader," I hear Maria complaining. "So far all he's had us do is dig."

"Digging's not so bad," Anahi says. "I'm getting really good at making holes."

"I caught a pencil-tailed tree mouse while I was digging," Tito says. "He was delicious."

Eduardo shakes his head and wags his tail.

"I didn't eat the tail part," Tito assures him. "Everyone knows you're not supposed to eat the tail."

"Hey, leader," Maria says. "How much longer do we have to dig?"

I don't answer her. I'm too busy *diggety-digging* another hole beside a tree to talk. *Diggety, dig, dig. Diggety, dig . . . Bonk.*

Suddenly a hard round thing falls onto my head. It looks like a ball. But it smells sweet. Like a fruit.

"Who threw that?" I ask.

Eduardo cocks his head.

"He doesn't know what you're talking about," Tito explains. "Neither do I."

"We've been too busy digging to throw anything," Maria grumbles.

Bonk. Down comes another one.

This fruit-smelling ball lands closer to my tail.

"Cut it out!" I shout.

Bonk. Bonk. Bonk.

Three more fruit-smelling balls fly down from the tree.

Tito looks up. "The howler monkeys are up there." He laughs. "Every time they swing between the branches, they knock down a passion fruit." He stuffs one of the passion-fruit balls in his mouth and takes a bite. "Yum!"

"What's a howler monkey?" I wonder.

HOWL!

Suddenly I hear some loud noises coming from up in the trees. It sounds sort of like someone is growling and laughing at the same time. But it sure isn't a dog laugh. It's too crazy. And way too loud. Louder than Maria, even!

I look up. Another passion-fruit ball flies down from the tree. It rolls down a hill—just like any ball would.

My tail starts wagging. My paws start hopping.

I know I'm supposed to be digging. But I can't help myself. When I see a ball roll by, I just have to fetch it!

The next thing I know, I'm running after that rolling passion fruit.

My paws run, run, run. The passion fruit rolls, rolls, rolls.

Run, run, run.

Roll, roll, roll.

"GOTCHA!" I snag that ball between my teeth and run back to the tree. "I fetched the ball!" I call up to the howler monkeys.

The howler monkeys just howl something back. They are so loud, they make my ears hurt.

"I really don't know what they're laughing about," Maria grumbles. "It's not like their home up there is any safer than ours is down here."

"They're not laughing," Anahi tells her. "They're trying to scare us away from their tree. I don't think they like sharing their fruit."

"That's because pretty soon there may not be any fruit left to share," Maria complains.

Eduardo rolls over onto his back. I know that trick. I learned it in dog school. It's called playing dead.

"Yeah," Tito agrees. "How long before that tree gets knocked down with the rest of them? I sure will miss the taste of passion fruit when that happens."

I take a bite of the passion-fruit ball I just fetched. *Mmmm.* It's sweet.

"Why would two-legs want to get rid of a tree that makes something so yummy?" I wonder.

"Don't ask me," Anahi says. "I don't understand anything two-legs do."

"Yeah," Maria snarls at me. "You explain it. *You're* the two-leg lover."

She makes that sound like a bad thing. But that's because she doesn't know any two-legs like *Josh.*

Just then, a howler monkey lets out a shout. It's loud and scary.

Bonk!

Another passion fruit hits me—right on the head.

"Hey!" I shout up to the howler monkeys. "That one hurt!"

The howler monkeys howl. My ears fold up on top of my head. The howling hurts them. And every time the monkeys let out a shout, another fruit falls.

Howl!

Bonk!

Howl!

Bonk!

"Okay," I yell back to the howler monkeys. "You don't have to tell me again. I'm out of here!"

I run off toward another tall, tall tree. One that looks just as tall as the first tree I saw when I got here.

Maybe that grassy field is on the other side of this tree.

Maybe I'm almost back where I started.

Maybe I will find . . .

Uh-oh! What's this? There's something sticky on my snout. And in my fur.

I'm caught in a net. A big, sticky net. It's holding me tight. I can't move. I'm sticky. And STUCK!

Wiggle, waggle, yikes! I'm in trouble!

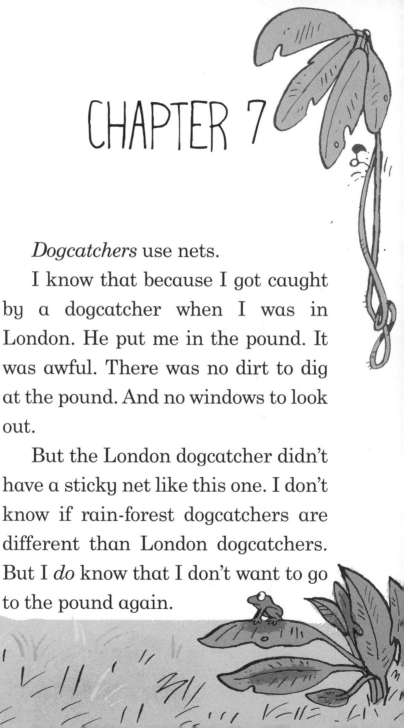

CHAPTER 7

Dogcatchers use nets.

I know that because I got caught by a dogcatcher when I was in London. He put me in the pound. It was awful. There was no dirt to dig at the pound. And no windows to look out.

But the London dogcatcher didn't have a sticky net like this one. I don't know if rain-forest dogcatchers are different than London dogcatchers. But I *do* know that I don't want to go to the pound again.

I have to get out of this net!

I push my head forward, but I can't break through.

I twist to the side. Sticky-net strings wrap around me.

I twist to the other side. Sticky-net strings pull even tighter.

And then, suddenly, strange eight-leg creatures start creeping and crawling all over me.

"Get off me, eight-legs!" I shout. "What do you want?"

Then I start to laugh—even though this isn't funny. I can't help it. Their creepy-crawling legs tickle.

I try to *shakity, shake, shake* the creepy crawlers off me. But they don't leave. They keep creeping and crawling.

Shakity, shake, shake.

Creepy-crawl. Tickle, tickle.

Every time I shake, the net gets tighter around me.

And then, suddenly, I hear . . .

"SPARKY! RUN!"

It's Maria. She's shouting as loud as she can. Not howler-monkey loud, but still pretty loud.

"GET OUT OF THERE!" she yells.

"I'm trying," I yell back.

"That cat is going to come for you!" Maria says. "You have to run away!"

That's weird. Why would I run

from a cat? I know all about cats. There's one named Queenie who lives near Josh and me. Queenie's mean. And she likes to tease me. But she's not scary. I don't have to run away just because some cat . . .

Uh-oh!

I turn my head. And that's when I see a spotted cat. Even though she's standing far away, I can see that she's nothing like Queenie. This cat is *huge.*

The cat opens her mouth. Even from back here, I can tell she's got the biggest, sharpest teeth I've ever seen.

Maria's right! I have to get out of here before that big cat eats me!

I twist and turn harder and harder inside the net. But I can't break free.

I punch at it with my paws, but the sticky string won't budge.

The spotted cat opens her mouth. Then she lets out a noise. It's not a purr like Queenie makes. This is a loud, angry growl.

"HELP!" I shout. "Somebody get me out of here!"

The next thing I know, Eduardo is at my side. He's using his bush-dog teeth to tear away the net.

Why didn't I think of that? I start to bite at the sticky net, too.

Yuck! One of the creepy crawlers creepy-crawls right into my mouth. Then it creepy-crawls all the way down my throat and into my belly. I feel all of its eight legs tickling my insides.

But I don't stop tearing at the sticky net. And neither does Eduardo.

GRRRRR . . . I hear the giant spotted cat growl again.

But Eduardo doesn't leave me. He just keeps tearing and tearing at the net.

And then . . . the net breaks! There's a huge hole.

Eduardo runs off. I follow close behind. I have to. Now I'm hearing

leaves rustling behind
me. The cat is running.
And, boy, is she fast.

Eduardo and I run.
Fast. Faster. *Fastest.*

The leaves *rustle, rustle,
rustle* behind me. The cat is getting
close. She runs a lot faster than
we do.

Suddenly, Eduardo stops running.

"Eduardo, what are you doing?" I
gasp. "Don't you hear the cat?"

Eduardo doesn't answer. He looks
down at a big, fat piece of tree that

has fallen down . . . and crawls inside!

Uh-oh! Eduardo is smaller than I am. I don't know if I can fit inside a tree. I've never tried.

Rustle, rustle, rustle.

From the sound of the leaves, I can tell that the big cat is almost here! I have to try to get inside the tree. I squish my belly up as tight as I can. I fold my paws under me. I crawl and squish myself inside, too.

I sure hope the cat can't hear my heart *thumpety, thump, thumping.* Because it's thumping louder than it ever has.

Quietly, we listen for the cat. We don't hear anything.

And then . . .

HOWL!

That howling is so loud. It can only come from one creature—a howler monkey!

PLUNK!

Just then, something plunks down on top of our hiding place. I wonder if it's that big cat.

PLUNK.

I hold my breath. I don't want that cat to even hear me breathing. I want her to keep going away. Far, far away.

HOWL!

The howler monkey lets out another loud noise.

Rustle, rustle, rustle. Leaves are rustling all around the fallen tree in which Eduardo and I are hiding.

I wonder if that sound is being made by the cat running past. It's scary not being able to see what's going on out there.

Rustle, rustle . . .

And then, the rustling stops. So does the howling. I don't hear anything at all.

Pushity, push, push.

Suddenly, I feel something pushing at my nose.

Gulp. What's going on now?

Pushity, push, push.

Oh wait. I know what that is!

It's Eduardo's rear end backing up into me. Does he want me to sniff hello? NOW? This is no time for sniffing!

But Eduardo keeps pushing. My paws start moving backward.

Now I get it. The cat is gone, and Eduardo wants to get out of this tree.

Slowly, I back out. My tail goes first. Then my belly. Then my head.

I take a big gasp of fresh, wet, hot air. It feels good to be out of the inside of a fallen tree.

Eduardo seems happy to be outside, too. His tail is wagging.

"Thank you," I whisper to him.

Eduardo smiles and nods his head. I guess he's saying, "You're welcome."

"THERE YOU ARE!"

That voice is loud. And a little scary. But I'm not afraid. I know it's Maria.

She, Anahi, and Tito all peek out

from behind some trees.

"Sparky, you're all right," Anahi says. She nuzzles me with her nose. "I'm so glad!"

"Thanks to Eduardo," I tell her. "He kept me from being a cat's dinner."

I can't believe I'm saying that. Everything is so strange here in the rain forest.

The logs have sharp teeth. The dogcatchers have eight legs and they build their own sticky nets. The cats are bigger than the dogs. And the two-legs are mean.

"It's getting dark," Maria says. "We should probably go home."

"Yeah," Tito agrees. "Maybe we can catch a nice dinner. Everyone knows the tastiest treats come out when it's dark."

Maria is right. The sun is disappearing. The day is almost over.

I wonder if Josh is home yet.

I wonder if he's sad that I'm not there to bark hello and lick his face.

I wonder if he feels as scared and all alone as I do.

Except I'm not alone. I have my bush-dog friends.

I haven't been a very good friend to them, though. I almost got Eduardo eaten by a cat. I can't ask them to help me find my bone. It's too dangerous.

"Come on, Sparky," Anahi says. She nudges me with her nose. "Let's go back to the lair."

I nod. I start to follow her back to

the house with no windows or doors. I will live in the bush dogs' house. But I don't know if it's ever going to feel like home.

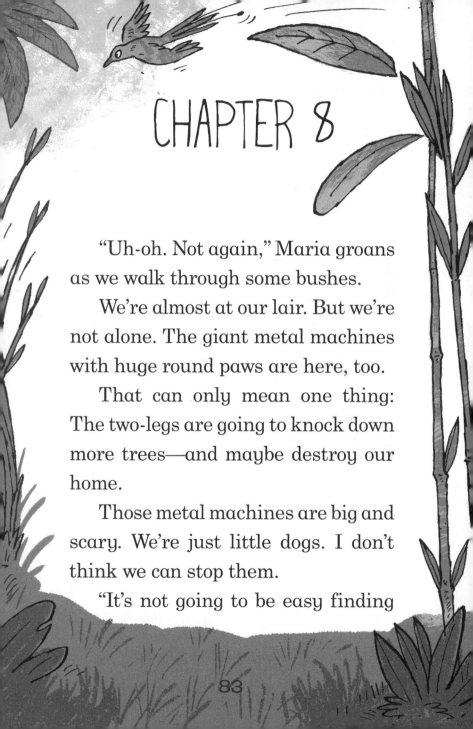

CHAPTER 8

"Uh-oh. Not again," Maria groans as we walk through some bushes.

We're almost at our lair. But we're not alone. The giant metal machines with huge round paws are here, too.

That can only mean one thing: The two-legs are going to knock down more trees—and maybe destroy our home.

Those metal machines are big and scary. We're just little dogs. I don't think we can stop them.

"It's not going to be easy finding

another abandoned armadillo nest to live in," Anahi says.

Eduardo shakes his head. He starts walking into the jungle.

"He says we better start looking," Tito explains.

We walk a few feet. Then Anahi stops in her tracks. "Will you look at that?" she says.

"What are they doing?" Maria wonders.

Eduardo cocks his head. I guess he's wondering the same thing. We all are.

A group of two-legs stands right in front of a big tree. They've linked their paws together. The way they are standing kind of makes them look like the fence that goes around

the backyard I share with Josh.

They're a great, big two-leg fence!

Not far from the two-leg fence surrounding the tall, tall tree, there's a field. It's covered in soft green grass.

I know that field. I played ball with two-legs on that field. Which can mean only one thing!

This tree—the one surrounded by the two-legs—is the tree near where I hid my bone.

I race over to the tree.

"Sparky, where are you going?" Maria asks. "Stay away from the two-legs!"

But I don't listen. I just start *diggety, dig, digging.* Dirt flies everywhere. Some of the two-legs cough when dirt hits them. But they still don't move.

And I keep digging until . . .

THERE IT IS! My bone. My beautiful magic bone. It's right there—waiting to take me home.

But before I can take a big bite, the two-legs in the metal machines leap out. They yell at the two-legs who have formed a fence.

The two-legs who are surrounding

the tree do not move. They just stand and stare at the two-legs who were in the metal machines.

The two-legs who were in the metal machines stare back at them. They yell some more. And then . . .

The yelling two-legs get back in their metal machines! They go away. They won't be knocking down any trees or destroying any dog lairs today!

"Wow!" Anahi exclaims. "Those two-legs standing there just saved our home."

"I've never seen two-legs do anything that nice," Tito says.

"See?" I say. "Some two-legs are really great."

"I guess so," Maria agrees.

Just then, Eduardo walks right

over to the two-leg fence.

"Eduardo, what are you doing?" Tito asks him nervously. "Come back here."

But Eduardo keeps walking. He stops in front of them, cocks his head, and smiles. And then . . .

"Thank you, two-legs," he says.

I can't believe my ears. "I didn't know you could talk," I tell him.

"I can," Eduardo says. "I just don't unless I have something important to say. And that was important."

"It really was," I say.

Just then, the two-legs start hitting their paws together. *Clap. Clap. Clap.*

Then some of the two-legs pull out tiny boxes. They aim them right at Eduardo.

Oh no! What are the two-legs
doing?

"Don't hurt my friend," I shout to
the two-legs.

Flash! Flash! Flash!

Flashes of light pop out of the
boxes.

Flash! Flash! Flash!

The lights hurt my eyes. I'm seeing spots, like the ones on the giant cat. The spots are scary.

Maria, Anahi, and Tito run and hide behind a big bush. But Eduardo doesn't move. He just stands there, smiling at the two-legs.

Finally the clapping stops. The flashing stops. And the two-legs start to walk away.

Once the two-legs are gone, the other bush dogs come out from behind the big bush. They walk over to where Eduardo and I are standing.

"Wow! Eduardo, you were really brave," Anahi tells him. "I never could have walked up to the two-legs like that. I would have been too scared."

"Me too," Tito agrees.

Maria shrugs. "You took a chance," she says. "You were lucky."

"Maybe," Eduardo tells her. "But it had to be said."

None of the bush dogs can argue with that.

We're all quiet for a minute. Then I tell them, "I've got to go home and see *my* two-leg. He's going to be sad if I'm not there to lick his face and chew his socks."

The bush dogs look at me.

"What are socks?" Tito asks. "Is

that some sort of food where you come from?"

I laugh. Tito sure loves to eat!

Anahi looks sadly at me. "You can't go," she says. "You're our leader!"

"You'll be okay," I promise her. "Your house is safe. And maybe you won't be so afraid of all two-legs, now that Eduardo has led the way."

I stop for a minute and *thinkety, think, think*.

"Eduardo would make a great new leader of your pack," I say finally. "He's the bravest of any of us. He saved me from that big cat. And he wasn't afraid to go near the two-legs, either."

Eduardo puffs up his chest.

"That would work," Anahi says.

"A leader doesn't have to talk a lot. He just has to be brave, keep us safe, and help us find food."

"Yeah," Tito agrees. "Eduardo is a really good hunter. He knows where all the best food hides. I'd follow him on a hunt."

We all look at Maria. She shrugs. "Okay," she says finally. "Eduardo's the leader."

"Great!" I look down at my magic bone. It's ready to take me home. "Good-bye, bush dogs," I say. "It was nice meeting you."

"Good-bye, Sparky," Tito, Maria, and Anahi all say at once.

Eduardo just nods. I guess he's done talking.

I take one last look at the Amazon Rain Forest. And then I chomp down on my magic bone. Hard!

Wiggle, waggle, whew. I feel dizzy—like my insides are spinning all around—but my outsides are standing still. Stars are twinkling in front of my eyes—even though it's daytime! All around me I smell food—fried chicken, salmon, roast beef. But there isn't any food in sight.

And then . . .

Kaboom! Kaboom! Kaboom!

Wiggle, waggle, woo-hoo! My kitchen! I'm back in my kitchen. In my house. A *real* house. With windows. And doors.

I run out of my door—the *doggie* door—and into the yard. I have to bury my bone to keep it safe.

I rush right over to Josh's flower garden. Then I start to *diggety, dig, dig*. I dig fast. It's cold. I don't want to be out here long.

That's a big hole. I drop my bone in. Then I *pushity, push, push* the cold dirt back over my bone until it's completely hidden.

Vroom. Vroom.

I hear something! It's a metal machine. And it's getting closer to my house. That can only mean one thing.

JOSH IS HOME!

I *zoomity, zoom, zoom* back into the house through my doggie door. Then I run to the front of the house and wait for Josh to open the big door.

My tail is wagging, hard. It can't wait to see Josh. Which is strange, because my tail doesn't have eyes.

The door opens, and there he is!

"JOSH! JOSH! JOSH!" I bark. I leap up so I can lick his face. "JOSH! JOSH! JOSH!" I'm so happy to be back with my two-leg.

Josh smiles and walks toward the kitchen. I follow close behind. There's food in the kitchen. Maybe he will give me some.

Josh stops suddenly. He looks down at the floor.

I look down at the floor.

There's a little green creature with a long tail and four little legs crawling in our kitchen! Where did he come from?

Josh bends down and picks up the little green four-leg. He looks at him. Then he looks at me.

"Don't look at me, Josh," I say. "I didn't bring him here. I've never seen him before."

Josh smiles at the little green four-leg.

Uh-oh. That means he likes him. Does he like him more than me?

I watch as Josh puts the green four-leg in a big, clear bowl.

Then he reaches into a bag on the counter. I love the sound of a bag being opened. *Crinkle, crinkle, crinkle.*

That sound means TREATS!

I jump up and grab the treat from Josh's hand.

The bush dogs might love to eat their agoutis in the jungle. But I'll take a tasty treat from a bag anytime.

Especially if that treat comes from Josh. Because he's the best there is.

Fun Facts about Sparky's Adventures in the Amazon Rain Forest

Amazon Rain Forest

The Amazon Rain Forest is the largest rain forest in the world. It is home to one-tenth of all mammals, and one-fifth of all plant and bird species. There are also two and a half million different types of insects!

Many animals in the rain forest have become endangered because of people cutting down trees, which destroys the homes in which the animals live and the food they eat. Today, thanks to action from people all over the world, laws are being put in place to stop the cutting down of trees in the Amazon Rain Forest. This will save the lives of many animals.

Bush Dogs

These South American dogs are rarely seen by people because they spend at least half their days in underground burrows. Their paws are webbed, which makes it easier for them to swim and dig for prey. Bush dogs are endangered because for many years people have been destroying the rain-forest habitats in which they live and hunt.

webbed
paws

Howler Monkeys

There's no sound in the rain forest quite as loud as the howl of the howler monkey. Its call can be heard three miles away! Howler monkeys use their loud voices to scare off other monkeys and animals who might want to climb or eat in their trees. Howler monkeys' tails are so strong, they hang by them alone. The underside of a howler monkey's tail has no fur. The howler can use that part of its tail to feel things, the way humans use the palms of their hands.

Social Spiders

Lately, groups of spiders have been causing a lot of trouble in Brazil. Thousands of spiders have been joining together to make massive webs that can be as big as nine feet wide! When the wind blows, the spiderwebs are carried away in the air. Then, when the wind dies down, the spiders fall to the ground. That makes it seem like it is actually raining spiders!

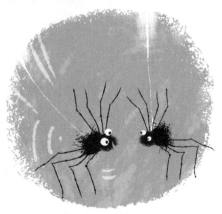

Ocelots

These members of the cat family are not often seen because they are awake at night, when they can do most of their hunting in the dark. They spend their days sleeping in trees or hidden in bushes. Ocelots like to eat rodents, small deer, birds, snakes, and fish. Until recently, ocelots were in danger because the trees in which they live and the bushes in which they hunt were being destroyed. Hunters also killed these beautiful cats for their spotted coats. However, Brazil has begun planting more trees and creating nature preserves where ocelots can roam freely without fear of being hunted.

About the Author

Nancy Krulik is the author of more than 200 books for children and young adults, including three *New York Times* Best Sellers. She is best known for being the author and creator of several successful book series for children, including Katie Kazoo, Switcheroo; How I Survived Middle School; and George Brown, Class Clown. Nancy lives in Manhattan with her husband, composer Daniel Burwasser, and her crazy beagle mix, Josie, who manages to drag her along on many exciting adventures without ever leaving Central Park.

About the Illustrator

You could fill a whole attic with Seb's drawings! His collection includes some very early pieces made when he was four—there is even a series of drawings he did at the movies in the dark! When he isn't doodling, he likes to make toys and sculptures, as well as bows and arrows for his two boys, Oscar and Leo, and their numerous friends. Seb is French and lives in England.

His website is www.sebastienbraun.com.

Dig up other

MAGIC BONE

books!

NANCY KRULIK

MAGIC BONE

BE CAREFUL WHAT YOU SNIFF FOR

NANCY KRULIK

MAGIC BONE

CATCH THAT DOG WAVE

NANCY KRULIK

MAGIC BONE

NICE SNOWING YOU!

NANCY KRULIK

MAGIC BONE

FOLLOW THAT FURBALL

NANCY KRULIK

MAGIC BONE

GO FETCH!

George Brown, Class Clown

Katie Kazoo, Switcheroo

Katie Kazoo
SWITCHEROO
Oh, Baby!

by Nancy Krulik • illustrated by John & Wendy

Katie Kazoo
SWITCHEROO
Out to Lunch

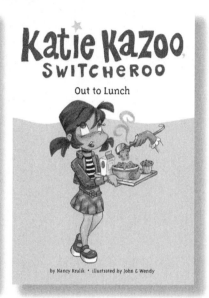

by Nancy Krulik • illustrated by John & Wendy

Katie Kazoo,
SWITCHEROO
Anyone But Me

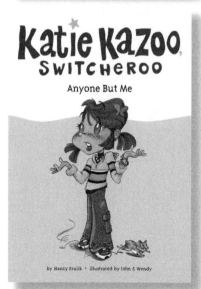

by Nancy Krulik • illustrated by John & Wendy

Katie Kazoo,
SWITCHEROO
Super Special Switcheroo!
All's Fair

by Nancy Krulik • illustrated by John & Wendy